the **BAD GUYS**

in

DO-YOU-THINK-
HE-SAURUS?!

TEXT AND ILLUSTRATIONS COPYRIGHT © 2018 BY AARON BLABEY

ALL RIGHTS RESERVED. PUBLISHED BY SCHOLASTIC INC., *PUBLISHERS SINCE 1920.* 557 BROADWAY, NEW YORK, NY 10012. scholastic AND ASSOCIATED LOGOS ARE TRADEMARKS AND/OR REGISTERED TRADEMARKS OF SCHOLASTIC INC. THIS EDITION PUBLISHED UNDER LICENSE FROM SCHOLASTIC AUSTRALIA PTY LIMITED. FIRST PUBLISHED BY SCHOLASTIC AUSTRALIA PTY LIMITED IN 2018.

THE PUBLISHER DOES NOT HAVE ANY CONTROL OVER AND DOES NOT ASSUME ANY RESPONSIBILITY FOR AUTHOR OR THIRD-PARTY WEBSITES OR THEIR CONTENT.

NO PART OF THIS PUBLICATION MAY BE REPRODUCED, STORED IN A RETRIEVAL SYSTEM, OR TRANSMITTED IN ANY FORM OR BY ANY MEANS, ELECTRONIC, MECHANICAL, PHOTOCOPYING, RECORDING, OR OTHERWISE, WITHOUT WRITTEN PERMISSION OF THE PUBLISHER. FOR INFORMATION REGARDING PERMISSION, WRITE TO SCHOLASTIC AUSTRALIA, AN IMPRINT OF SCHOLASTIC AUSTRALIA PTY LIMITED, 345 PACIFIC HIGHWAY, LINDFIELD NSW 2070 AUSTRALIA.

THIS BOOK IS A WORK OF FICTION. NAMES, CHARACTERS, PLACES, AND INCIDENTS ARE EITHER THE PRODUCT OF THE AUTHOR'S IMAGINATION OR ARE USED FICTITIOUSLY, AND ANY RESEMBLANCE TO ACTUAL PERSONS, LIVING OR DEAD, BUSINESS ESTABLISHMENTS, EVENTS, OR LOCALES IS ENTIRELY COINCIDENTAL.

ISBN 978-1-338-18961-2

10 9 8 7 6 5 4 3 2 1   18 19 20 21 22

PRINTED IN THE U.S.A.   23
FIRST U.S. PRINTING 2018

· AARON BLABEY ·

the BAD GUYS

in

DO-YOU-THINK-
HE-SAURUS?!

SCHOLASTIC INC.

THIS was the arranged
LANDING POINT.

THIS is where Mr. Wolf and the boys
were supposed to return to Earth.

So, *where are they?*

· CHAPTER 1 ·
RIGHT PLACE, WRONG TIME

65 MILLION YEARS EARLIER . . .

OK.

So, let me get this straight . . .

We were on our way to

SAVE EARTH

from an **ALIEN INVASION,**

but our escape pod turned out to be a

TIME MACHINE

so *instead*, we ended up in

the distant past surrounded by

DINOSAURS.

Did I get
that *right*?!

WINK!

Wolf, they can TOTALLY see you . . .

You'd *think* that, wouldn't you?
But NO! I'm *completely invisible*.

Isn't it amazing?

Wolfie!
You're thinking of the
TYRANNOSAURUS REX.
These are **VELOCIRAPTORS.**
And they can TOTALLY
see you.

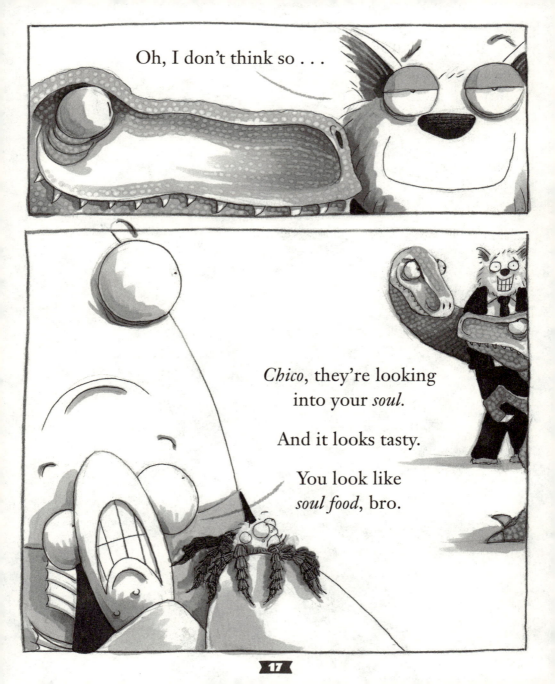

Hmm, I know it looks that way . . . But I'm *pretty* confident if I just keep really still I'll be perfectly—

SNAP!!

AARRRGGGHHHH!!!

Well, *amigos . . .*
in Bolivia we have an old saying—

*It's better to be eaten by dinosaurs
than it is to be eaten by aliens
with butts for hands.*

That is *SO* not an old
Bolivian saying.

No.
No, it's not.

Nevertheless,
we're doomed.

I want you to know—I've
loved working with you guys.

I just feel sad we didn't really
get to save the world.

Don't feel sad yet, soldier . . .

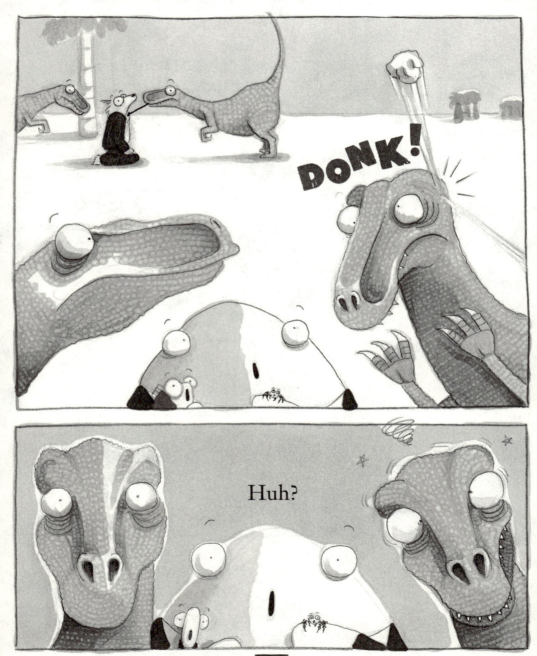

· CHAPTER 2 ·
GONE ROGUE

FOOMP!

Shhhhhhh . . .

Don't. Make.
A. Sound.

This way.
Stay close . . .

TUMBLE!

TUMBLE!

VOOSH!

Snake?!

Where are we going?

We have to get back to the
time-machine-thingy and get it working!

WE are the only ones who know

what's coming—the world is about to be

DESTROYED

BY ALIENS but we are

65 MILLION YEARS

away from the action!

WHAT ARE WE GOING
TO DO?!

THIS is what we're going to do— we're going to DEAL WITH IT. **WOLF UP,** soldier! Right now!

We're going to save the world. *Say it!*

We're going to save the world . . .

And **THIS** is how it's going to go down . . .

Done.

Good.
Now, Tree?
Move silently through
the jungle and get us to

HIGH GROUND.

I need to see the
lay of the land.

Yes, sir!

Who *are* you?!
And what have
you done with
Mr. Snake?

· CHAPTER 3 ·
SO MANY PROBLEMS

Chico?
With respect,
what you're trying to do is

LOCO...

This thing
zapped us millions of years
into the past by flying
SUPER-CRAZY-FAST.
How can it send us BACK if it's broken?

Hmmm, well, that's the thing— it got us **BACK TO EARTH** by moving us quickly, so yes, it definitely used

SPEED

to move us through **SPACE** . . .

But what I want to do is find the part of this contraption that moved us through

TIME.

That's a TOTALLY different thing. Don't you think?

Could you repeat the question?

Look—
this little space pod
blasted us down to Earth
from the moon and put us
exactly **WHERE** we need to be.
We're in exactly the right

PLACE.

BUT!

It also sent us 65 million years into the **PAST.**
And that's completely different.
Space. Time. Two separate things, right?
So there must be something in this pod that can

OPEN A WINDOW INTO THE FUTURE.

We just need to find it, open it, and *step through it.*
You hear what I'm saying?

So, all we need to do is identify the **TIME-TRAVEL DRIVE.** And if I had to guess . . .

I'd probably try to hot-wire this and . . .

BOOM!

Well, *that* looks promising!

Could this be . . .
a *doorway to the future?*

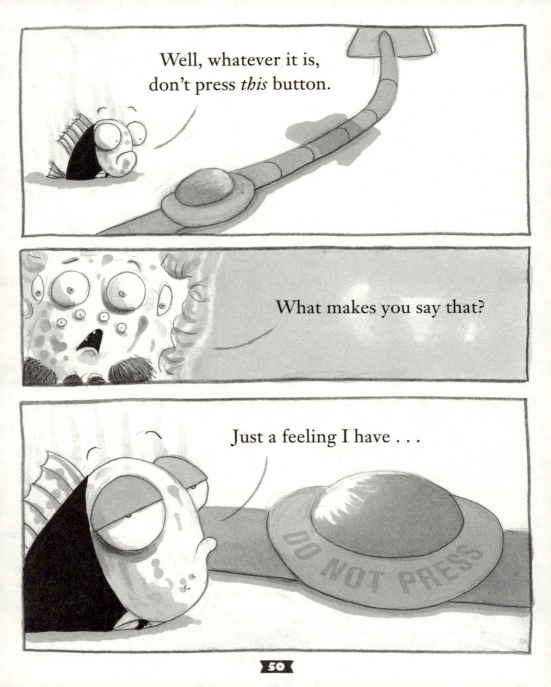

Well, whatever it is, don't press *this* button.
What makes you say that?
Just a feeling I have . . .
DO NOT PRESS

That **RING** . . .
Don't you think it looks like a portal?
Like a *portal through time*, perhaps?

I'll just nod my head and
hopefully you'll be struck by
lightning before you can ask me
any more stupid questions . . .

But if it is . . .
a . . .
por . . . tal . . .

Then what?

Look, I didn't really want
you to get struck by lightning,
OK?

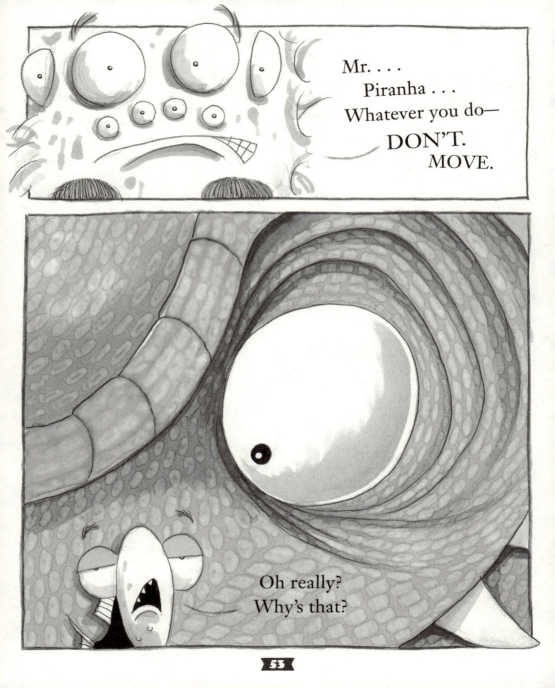

Wait—there isn't something
behind me, is there?

It's a *Tyrannosaurus rex*. Their vision IS based on movement, so if you stay completely still—

ZOOOOM!

AAARRRRGGGHHH!!!

You're going to *move around a whole lot.* THAT'S the key to success in this situation.

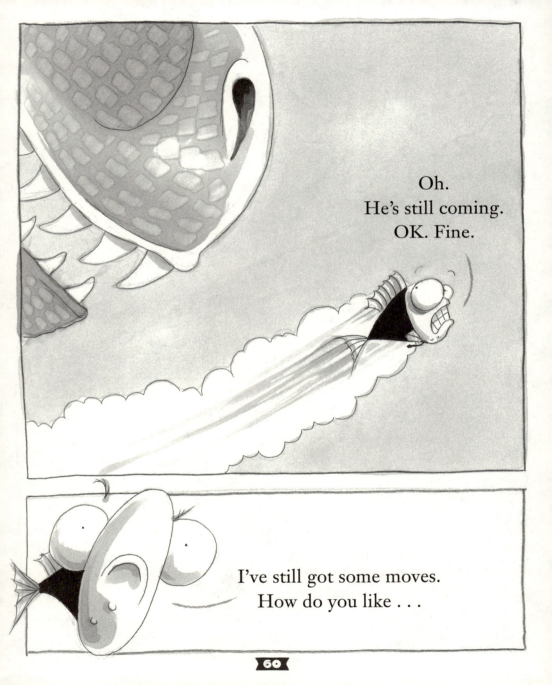

Oh.
He's still coming.
OK. Fine.

I've still got some moves.
How do you like . . .

OK.
I'm in deep poop.

Wait a minute!

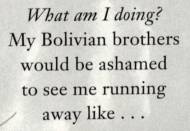

What am I doing?
My Bolivian brothers
would be ashamed
to see me running
away like . . .

. . . a jellyfish
with tiny little
baby pants.

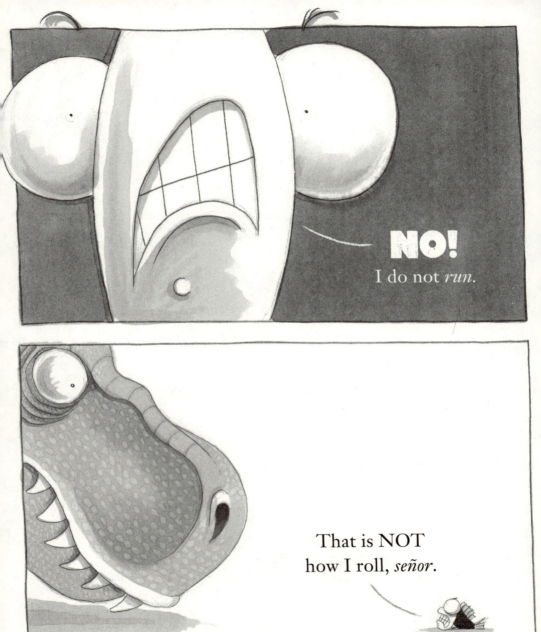

I bring the THUNDER!

I bring the
LIGHTNING!

I AM THE
PERFECT
STORM!

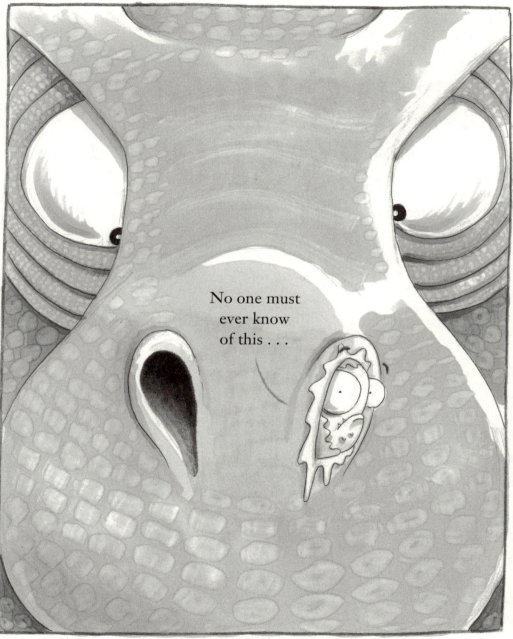

· CHAPTER 4 ·
WHO'S RUNNING THIS SHOW?

What can you see?

Shhh, keep it down!
Legs is playing around
with some kind of contraption.
Where'd he get that from?

I don't see Piranha
anywhere . . .

Really?!
We should go
look for him!
He might be
in trouble!

Oh man.
You're right
We *are* in trouble.

It's all right, though.
We'll get out of this,
I promise.
But I need you
to stay *calm*.

Listen to him, Wolfie.
He knows what he's
talking about.

You're right, Mr. Shark.

And you were right before—
it's almost like . . . our little team . . .
has a new . . . *leader*.

Isn't it? He he he.
Yeah.

Are you kidding?!
I don't want *your* job,
you hair-brained lunatic.
Who needs THAT
kind of responsibility?

I'm just your
wingman.

Your
vastly superior
wingman.

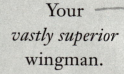

That was *too* close.

I sure hope Mr. Tarantula knows what he's doing.

· CHAPTER 5 ·
THE PORTAL

Soooo . . .
if I enter the date and
the coordinates, switch on
those three, bypass *that* one,
and reboot *this* one,
shouldn't that . . .

give me . . .

VOOF!
VOOF!
VOOF!
VOOF!
VOOF!

A VORTEX INTO ANOTHER DIMENSION?!

Yeah. Pretty sure that's what it is.

Yep . . .

PORTAL:

OPERATIONAL

LOOK!

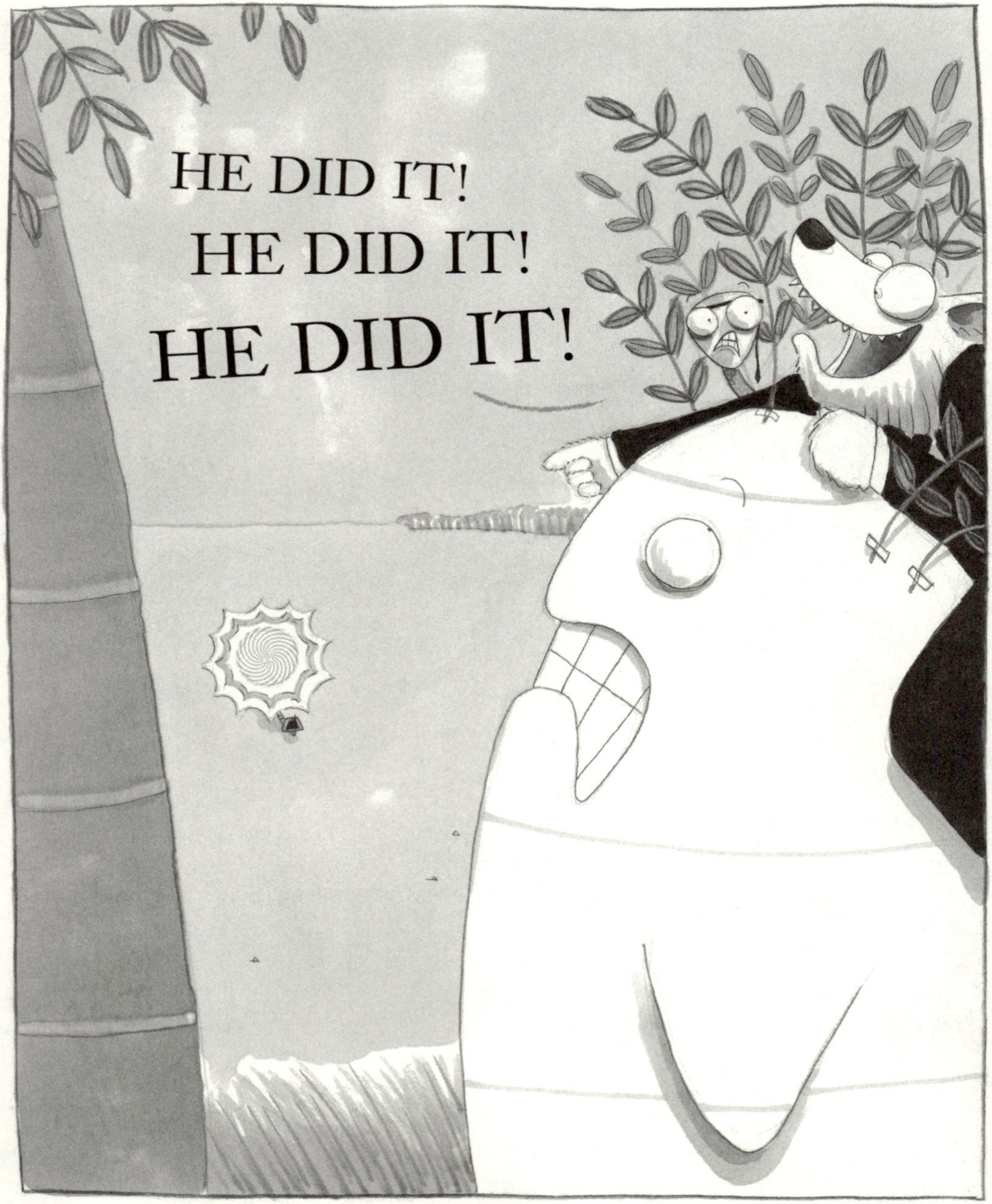
HE DID IT!
HE DID IT!
HE DID IT!

SHHHH! You'll give us away!

Oh my stars, I'm SO sorry.

Tree! Move *slowly* and *silently* away from this cliff top, back through the jungle, and down to the time machine . . .

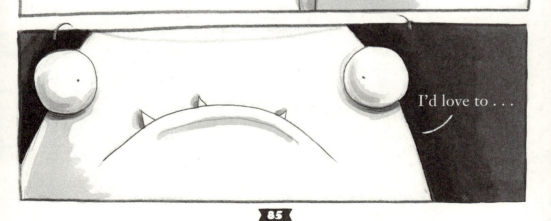

I'd love to . . .

But Mr. Wolf
just rang the

**DINNER
BELL!**

Look out!

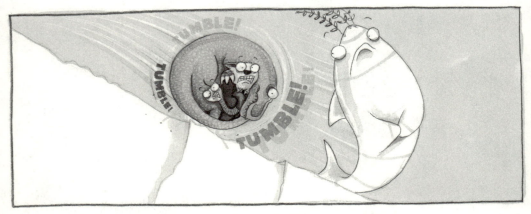

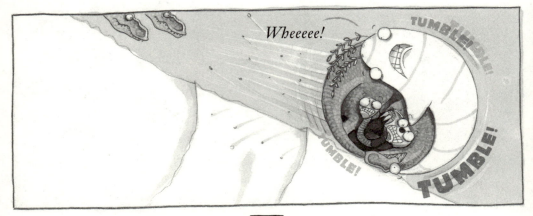

Wheeeee!

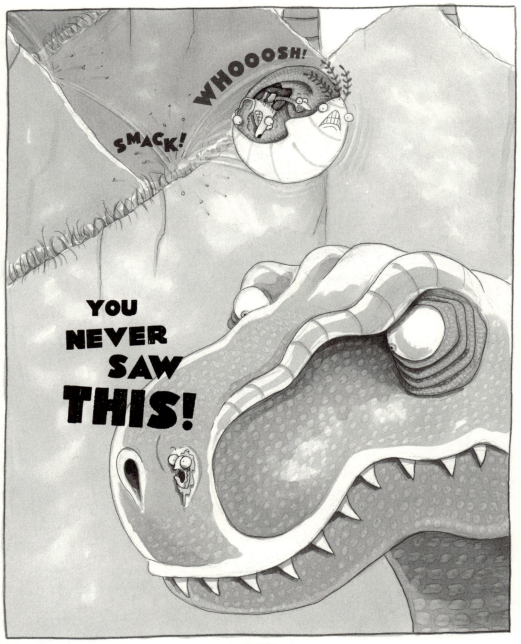

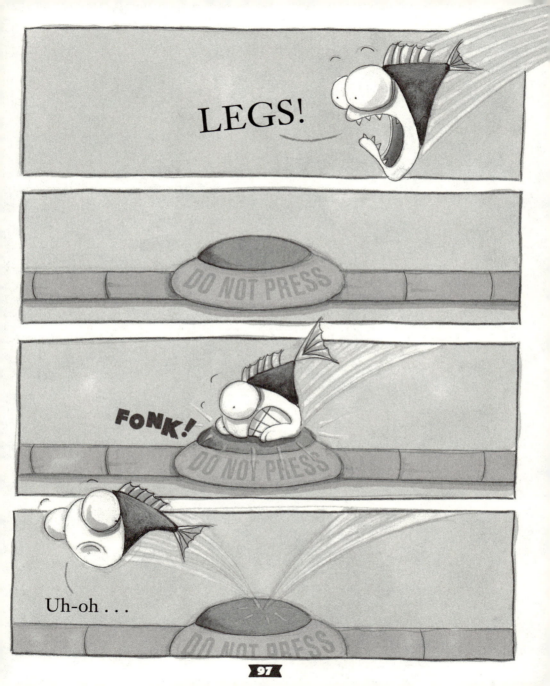

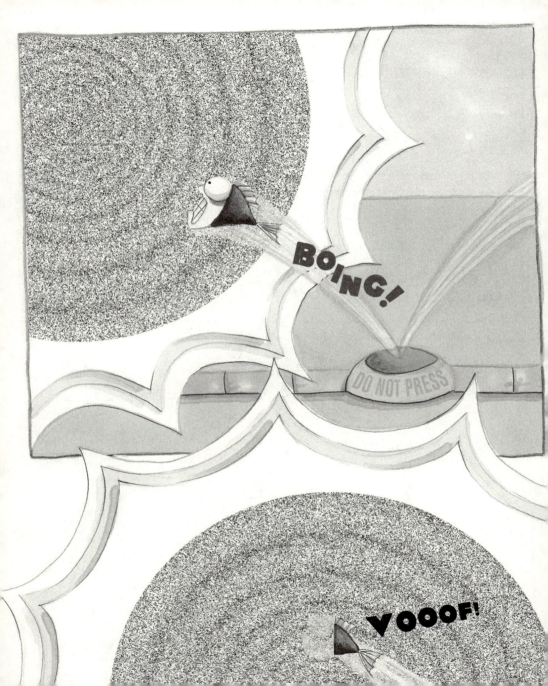

VOOOF!

CHAPTER 6

ONE—WAY TICKET TO WEIRD TOWN

WOW!

This is so beautiful!

And so *peaceful* . . .

Hmmm.

I wonder how the others are doing.

Do I look strange to you?

In what way?

I don't know.
I just don't feel
like myself . . .

Does anyone else feel

AWESOME?

What a pleasant journey.
Dude, that was just delightful.

But hey!
Look over there . . .
That looks just like . . .

· CHAPTER 7 ·
BACK TO THE . . . YOU KNOW

Mr. Wolf!
You're alive!

Agent Fox!
There are **ALIENS!**
I mean, Marmalade is . . .
I mean, THEY'RE COMING!

Mr. Wolf . . .
They're
already
here.

Oh no.

My goodness, what a *kerfuffle!*

I'm terribly sorry, but we haven't been formally introduced . . .

· CHAPTER 8 ·
HUH?!

Heavens!
That little chap was
certainly in a hurry!

Mr. Shark . . .
You're shape-shifting.

You think
that's cool?

Check this out . . .

SHUDDER!
SHUDDER!

Guys, I think Mr. Snake is lifting a car . . .
with his **MIND.**

Mr. Wolf?
I feel a little scared.
What's going on here, man?

I'm not sure,
buddy.

But if
I had to guess,

I'd say we've
got ourselves
some . . .

SUPERPOWERS?! Who saw THAT coming?!

THE BAD GUYS might have gotten an upgrade,

but does that *guarantee* them a place in

THE INTERNATIONAL LEAGUE OF **HEROES?**

Nope. But they will be holding **TRYOUTS...**

the **BAD GUYS** *in Superbad*

SPEEDING TO YOU SOON.

LIKE AN ENHANCED PIRANHA.

The following broadcast was picked
up by satellite, while being beamed
from Earth into deep space . . .

KDJFLOER
HGCOINW
ERUHCGLE
IRWFHEKLW
JFHXALHW!

PILOT EPISODE

*The Glamorous Life of
Dr. Rupert Marmalade*

Hiiiiiiii, everyone!
This is soooooooooo exciting!
My very own
REALITY TV SHOW!
I could just *die*.

But what's that, you say?
Who IS this disgusting
CUTE and **CUDDLY**
little creature calling himself
DR. RUPERT MARMALADE?
Well, I've only got one thing
to say about that . . .

SURPRISE!

It's me!

KDJFLOERHGCO INWERUHCGLEIR WFHEKLWJFHXALHW!

Did you miss me?!

Shut **UP**!

Of course you did.

I've been on an

INTERGALACTIC SHOPPING SPREE

and I was like
"*OMG, Earth? Yes, please!
I'll TAKE IT!*"

I just *had* to have it.

Sooooo . . .
THIS is my new planet!
Don't you just LOVE it?!

Let me show you around . . .

I've worked SO hard to make
it my own, you know?

I really wanted to, like, personalize it
and make a real statement with it.

I think it's just so "me."

And all the little creatures who lived here are mine now, too!

I RULE WITHOUT MERCY.

But at the same time,
I'm *super fun* to be around.
You know what I mean?
I'm SO complicated.

10 THINGS I LOOOOOVE!

1. Having my own planet

2. Showing no pity

3. Chocolate sprinkles

4. Feeling the fear of millions

5. Leading my invading army to victory

6. Annihilating my enemies

7. Cheese sticks

8. Intergalactic domination

9. Watching my enemies lose all hope

10. Skinny jeans

10 THINGS I TOTALLY HATE

1. Being called CUTE

2. Being called CUDDLY

3. Being called CUTE AND CUDDLY

4. Being called anything that implies I'm CUTE AND CUDDLY without actually saying it

5. Wolves, Sharks, Snakes, Piranhas, and Foxes
(*It's an Earth thing. But don't worry. It's TOTALLY under control.*)

6. Body hair (ugh)

7. Running out of cheese sticks

8. Books that end with the words "To be continued . . ."

9. The happiness of others

10. When a fart goes wrong

My *hopes and dreams?*

Well, I've already accomplished so much, you know? I'm rich. I'm *gorgeous*. I have a planet of my own, with a side order of **ABSOLUTE POWER.**

I've got it all.

So . . . I guess my dream is to wake up tomorrow being just as **PERFECT AS I AM TODAY.**

I think that's something we can ALL relate to.

Now, if you'll excuse me,
I have a busy day ahead of me—
I'm producing a movie version
of *the story of my life*.

It's called

HE'S JUST AMAZEBALLS.

I wrote the screenplay.
It's even better than it sounds.
We've hired some good-looking kid
to play me, but personally I don't think
anyone will have what it takes.

QUIET
ON SET

★ JUSTIN ★
BEAVER

DIRECTOR
STEVEN
SEALBERG

That dude is **SCARILY CONFIDENT**, huh? While he's busy getting **FAMOUS,** I'd rather curl up on the couch for some **GOOD OLD-FASHIONED FUN**. And what's more fun than a quiz? **WAIT!** Don't answer that! I promise these **GAMES** and **PUZZLES** really are bad-to-the-bone tests for **WANNABE HEROES!**

(Puzzle answers can be found on page 171.)

BAD GUYS TRYOUT

Are you brave enough to bungee jump into **DANGER**? Fearless enough to face a laser cannon's **DEADLY** rays? Wily enough to withstand a **ZOMBIE KITTEN ATTACK**? Take this quiz to find out if you have what it takes to join the **BAD GUYS** on their next mission!

1. A **THIEF** is robbing a bank across town. You must act **QUICKLY**, or he'll get away. How do you get there?

   A. Ride a motorcycle—it's great for taking shortcuts.
   B. Drive a monster truck—you'll crush anything that gets in your way.
   C. Steal a rocket ship—you'll have it back by lunch.
   D. Walk—nothing is safer than the two-foot express.

2. What kind of **JOB** would you like to have when you **GROW UP**?

   A. A librarian
   B. A superhero
   C. An astronaut
   D. A firefighter

3. The circus is in town! But something **SMELLS ROTTEN** under the **BIG TOP**. To find out what is going on, you need to sneak in. What is your **DISGUISE**?

A. A tightrope walker—you aren't afraid of heights.
B. A clown—no one will see past the big red nose.
C. Who needs a disguise? You're wearing clean pants!
D. A lion tamer—all eyes will be on the cat.

4. What is your favorite **WEEKEND ACTIVITY**?

A. Skydiving without a parachute
B. Watching cartoons at home
C. All-you-can-eat burrito buffet
D. Playing laser tag

5. You are stranded on a **DESERT ISLAND** when you find a **TREASURE CHEST**. What do you hope to find inside?

A. A fishing pole—you can catch your own dinner.
B. Red meat—you have always wanted to wrestle sharks.
C. Sunscreen—you don't want to burn.
D. A raft—sailing home won't be easy, but you are up for the challenge.

6. It's Monday morning—time for **SCHOOL**! But you can't turn in your homework. What's your excuse?

    A. It fell into the nest of a baby bird you rescued.

    B. Would never happen. You turned it in early.

    C. You wrote the answers in invisible ink.

    D. It contained dangerous information, so you blew it up.

7. What kind of **PET** would you like to have?

    A. A goldfish

    B. A bunny

    C. A pit bull

    D. A tiger

8. You are on a **SHIP** when it hits an iceberg and begins to sink. What do you do?

    A. Steer the ship toward dry land

    B. Dive underwater to plug the leaks

    C. Freeze the ocean with an arctic blast ray

    D. Run for a lifeboat

To find your score, add up the points for each of your answers:

1. A: 2, B: 3, C: 4, D: 1   5. A: 2, B: 4, C: 1, D: 3
2. A: 1, B: 4, C: 3, D: 2   6. A: 3, B: 1, C: 2, D: 4
3. A: 3, B: 2, C: 1, D: 4   7. A: 1, B: 2, C: 3, D: 4
4. A: 4, B: 1, C: 2, D: 3   8. A: 2, B: 3, C: 4, D: 1

Less than 10 points: BAD GUY-IN-TRAINING

You like to play it safe, which isn't a bad thing. But sometimes heroes have to take risks. If Mr. Shark can face his fear of tarantulas without shrieking like a baby, you can do the things that scare you most. Soon you'll be on your way to full Bad Guy status!

10 to 15 points: TEAM MEMBER

You are strong and reliable. Though you don't go looking for danger, you don't run from it, either. And just like Mr. Piranha, you never break down—you only break wind. You are silent, but deadly. So grab a burrito, get ready for a mission, and let a stinky one rip!

16 to 20 points: LEADER OF THE PACK

You are a true hero. There is no villain too vile, rescue too risky, or guinea pig too cute to stop you from saving the day. With nerves of steel and a take-charge attitude, guys like you and Mr. Wolf make perfect mission leaders. The only question is: Who will you save next?

More than 20 points: TOTAL MANIAC

You may be TOO brave! Daredevils like you are not afraid to scale skyscrapers without a net. But your enthusiasm can make you totally lose control. Like Mr. Snake, you may end up eating the chickens you are supposed to be rescuing. Don't be like Mr. Snake.

IT'S ALL IN THE DETAILS

Ay, caramba! That **NASTY** Dr. Marmalade used his Confusion Blaster 3000 to **BAFFLE**, **BEWILDER**, and **BAMBOOZLE** the Bad Guys.

Can you **SPOT** the **FIVE DIFFERENCES** between these two scenes?

LOOKING FOR TROUBLE

If you want to be a **BAD GUY**, you gotta have an eye for details. Search for the **WORDS** in this **PUZZLE**. Remember—they could be arranged left to right, top to bottom, or on a slant.

AGENT FOX
ALIENS
BAD GUYS
BURRITO
BUTT TENTACLES
CHICKENS
CUTE-ZILLA RAY

FARTS
GRANNY GUMBO
GUINEA PIG
HERMANO
HEROES
INTERGALACTIC
LEGS

MARMALADE
PIRANHA
SHARK
SNAKE
WOLF
ZITTENS

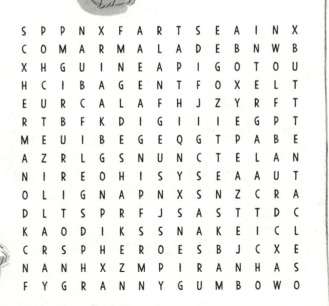

```
S P P N X F A R T S E A I N X
C O M A R M A L A D E B N W B
X H G U I N E A P I G O T O U
H C I B A G E N T F O X E L T
E U R C A L A F H J Z Y R F T
R T B F K D I G I I I E G P T
M E U I B E G E Q G T P A B E
A Z R L G S N U N C T E L A N
N I R E O H I S Y S E A A U T
O L I G N A P N X S N Z C R A
D L T S P R F J S A S T T D C
K A O D I K S S N A K E I C L
C R S P H E R O E S B J C X E
N A N H X Z M P I R A N H A S
F Y G R A N N Y G U M B O W O
```

MASTER OF DISGUISE

Whether you're dressing up as an adorable **KITTEN** or a futuristic **ROBOT**, a good disguise can help you blend in on undercover **MISSIONS.** Plus, sometimes it's just nice to feel pretty. Can you draw an **OUTFIT** on me that will hide my true identity?

CRACKING THE CODE

Dr. Marmalade is at it again! That sneaky villain is always trying to **DESTROY** the Bad Guys. We've **STOLEN** his notebook to find out what he is thinking, but his notes are written in **CODE**! Can you help me **UNCOVER** his hidden messages? Hint: **MARMALADE** is as <u>opposite</u> from the Bad Guys as can be. Some might even call him <u>backward</u>!

Code Letters	A	B	C	D	E	F	G	H	I	J	K	L	M	N	O	P	Q	R	S	T	U	V	W	X	Y	Z
Real Letters																										

CODED MESSAGES:

1: NB HVXIVG KOZM RH . . . HVXIVG.

2: TLGXSZ, YZW TFBH!

3: BLF XZM'G ULLO NV GSZG VZHROB.

4: R'N HL NFXS HNZIGVI GSZM BLF.

5: SVILVH? NLIV ORPV AVILVH!

6: BLF'OO MVEVI HGLK NV!

HISS-TERICALLY FUNNY

I know everyone thinks I'm a **GROUCH**, but I've got a lighter side, too. These jokes prove I'm a **FUNNY** guy. Just don't make a big hairy deal out of it!

Where did Mr. Wolf leave his **CAR**?
In the barking lot!

What is Mr. Shark's favorite
SANDWICH?
Peanut butter and jellyfish!

Where does Mr. Piranha keep his **MONEY**?
In the river-bank!

When would Agent Fox **SLEEP**
on the job?
When she goes undercover!

Why does Mr. Shark **SWIM**
in salt water?
Because pepper makes him sneeze!

When is it **BAD LUCK** to see Mr. Snake? *When you're chicken!*

How does Legs talk with other **SPIDERS**? *Though the World Wide Web!*

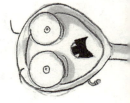

What did Mr. Wolf say when someone **STEPPED** on his toe? *Aoooowwww!*

Why doesn't Mr. Piranha play **BASKETBALL**? *He's afraid of the net!*

What was Mr. Snake's **FAVORITE** baby toy? *His rattle!*

How does a **HERO** drink water? *With just ice!*

DANGEROUS MAZE

Help the Bad Guys **SAVE** the day by finding your way through this twisted maze. And remember— **DANGER** lurks around every corner!

START

FINISH

ANSWER KEY

PAGE 162: IT'S ALL IN THE DETAILS

1. Traffic Light
2. Agent Fox's belt
3. Giraffe's spot
4. Telephone wire
5. Tire wheel

PAGE 164: LOOKING FOR TROUBLE

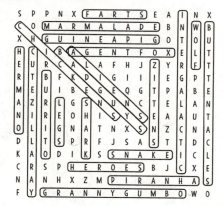

```
S P P N X F A R T S E A I N X
C O M A R M A L A D E B N W X
X H G U I N E A P I G O T O B
H C I B A G E N T F O X E L U
E U T R C A L A F H J Z Y F T
R T E I B F K D I G I I I E T
M Z I R U I S E Q G T I S P E
A I L R L G S N U N C T E A N
N L L I E O H T E S Y S L U T
O A A G N A T N X S I A A N A
D R R P D I K S N A K E Z T C
K A S H E R O E S B J C L L
C N A N H X Z M P I R A N H A E
N Y H G R A N N Y G U M B O W O
F Y
```

PAGE 166: CRACKING THE CODE

A	B	C	D	E	F	G	H	I	J	K	L	M	N	O	P	Q	R	S	T	U	V	W	X	Y	Z
Z	Y	X	W	V	U	T	S	R	Q	P	O	N	M	L	K	J	I	H	G	F	E	D	C	B	A

1: MY SECRET PLAN IS . . . SECRET.
2: GOTCHA, BAD GUYS!
3: YOU CAN'T FOOL ME THAT EASILY.
4: I'M SO MUCH SMARTER THAN YOU.
5: HEROES? MORE LIKE ZEROES!
6: YOU'LL NEVER STOP ME!

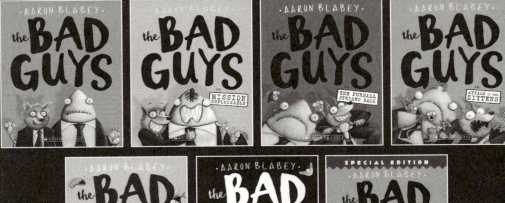